STORIES
FOR
EASTER

Look out for all of these enchanting
story collections by Enid Blyton

Animal Stories
Cherry Tree Farm
Christmas Stories
Christmas Tales
Christmas Treats
Christmas Wishes
Fireworks in Fairyland
Five-Minute Stories
Goodnight Stories
Magical Fairy Tales
Mr Galliano's Circus
Nature Stories
Pet Stories
Rainy Day Stories
Sleepytime Stories
Spellbinding Stories
Springtime Stories
Stories for Bedtime
Stories for Christmas
Stories of Magic and Mischief
Stories of Mischief Makers
Stories of Rotten Rascals
Stories of Spells and Enchantments
Stories of Tails and Whiskers
Stories of Wizards and Witches
Stories of Wonders and Wishes
Summer Adventure Stories
Summertime Stories
Tales of Tricks and Treats
The Wizard's Umbrella
Winter Stories

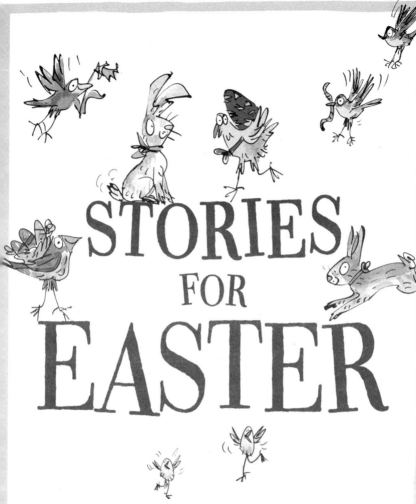

STORIES
FOR
EASTER

Enid Blyton

Illustrated by Mark Beech

h HODDER

HODDER CHILDREN'S BOOKS

Previously published in Great Britain in *The O'Clock Tales* in 2010 by Egmont UK Limited,
Springtime Stories in 2018 by Hodder & Stoughton Limited and
Stories for Every Season in 2019 by Hodder & Stoughton Limited
This collection first published in Great Britain in 2025 by
Hodder & Stoughton Limited

1 3 5 7 9 10 8 6 4 2

A CIP catalogue record for this book is available from the British Library.

ISBN 978 1 444 98021 9

Typeset in Cambria by Palimpsest Book Production Limited, Falkirk, Stirlingshire

Printed and bound in Great Britain by Clays Ltd, Elcograf S.p.A.

The paper and board used in this book are made from wood from responsible sources.

Hodder Children's Books
An imprint of
Hachette Children's Group
Part of Hodder & Stoughton
Carmelite House
50 Victoria Embankment
London EC4Y 0DZ

The authorised representative in the EEA is Hachette Ireland, 8 Castlecourt Centre,
Dublin 15, D15 XTP3, Ireland (email: info@hbgi.ie)

An Hachette UK Company
www.hachette.co.uk
www.hachettechildrens.co.uk

CONTENTS

The Witch's Egg   1

The Surprising Easter Egg   7

The Lonely Rabbit   18

The Easter Chickens   29

The Top of the Wall   37

Gillian and the Lamb   42

The Big Box of Chocolates   53

How Very Surprising!   70

The Big Juicy Carrot   83

Fairy Easter Eggs   92

The Blackbirds' Secret   114

The Blown-Away Rabbit   120

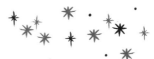

The Witch's Egg

Once upon a time Sneaky the elf peeped into Witch Upadee's kitchen and saw her working a spell. First she took a small chocolate Easter egg and put it on a plate. Sneaky knew the kind. You could buy them for a ha'penny each, and they were filled with sticky cream inside. He sat himself on the windowsill and watched to see what happened next.

Witch Upadee took a peacock's feather and stroked the tiny egg. Then she blew on it hard and chanted, 'Grow, grow. Quick and slow. Make yourself sweet for witches to eat. Grow, grow. Quick and slow!'

And, to Sneaky's enormous astonishment, that tiny chocolate egg began to grow big on the plate! How it grew! How it swelled up! My goodness, Sneaky did feel hungry when he saw that great egg of chocolate, all ready to be eaten, growing bigger and bigger! He nearly fell off the windowsill in surprise – and then, what a shock he got! Witch Upadee saw him and gave a shout of rage. She picked up her broom and swept him right off her windowsill!

'You nasty little sneaking thing, always

peeping and prying! Go away! You *shan't* see my spells!'

But Sneaky had seen enough. He ran home grinning and rubbing his hands. *He* would make a chocolate egg grow like that too – and my, what a lot of money he would make by selling it!

He bought a chocolate egg and took it home. He set it on a plate and then went to borrow a peacock's feather from his friend next door. He stroked the little egg with it, and then blew on it hard, feeling tremendously excited. Then he chanted loudly the magic song, 'Grow, grow. Quick and slow. Make yourself sweet for *fairies* to eat. Grow, grow. Quick and slow!'

The chocolate egg began to grow. How it grew! You really should have seen it. It was a most marvellous sight. First it was as big as a hen's egg. Then as big as a goose's. Then as big as a swan's. Then as large as an ostrich's. Then as big as a coal scuttle – and it went on growing. Sneaky was delighted. He danced around in joy, watching the egg grow.

It grew and it grew. Crack! It broke the plate with its weight. But Sneaky didn't mind. He could buy lots of new plates with the money for that lovely egg! Then the egg grew bigger than the table – and crack! One of the legs gave way, and down went the table and the egg too. But still it went on growing!

When it was as big as a large wheelbarrow, Sneaky thought it was big enough. After all, he had to get it out of the door and take it to market – it wouldn't do for it to get *too* big! So he shouted to it, 'Stop! Don't grow any more, egg!' But the egg didn't take a bit of notice, no, not a bit. It just went on growing – and however much Sneaky begged it to stop it simply wouldn't. Sneaky didn't know the right words to say, you see! Well, it grew – and it grew – and it grew – and at last it couldn't grow any more, because it was as big as the room itself – and poor Sneaky was squashed flat in one corner. And then, in pressing itself against the ceiling, the egg broke! Out came a great stream of sticky cream – all over poor Sneaky! After that the egg stopped growing, for the spell was broken.

But do you know – the only way Sneaky could get out of the room was by eating his way through the egg! It took him two days – and oh, the mess he was in! And now, if you meet a small elf who says he simply can't *bear* Easter eggs, just ask him his name. It's sure to be Sneaky!

The Surprising Easter Egg

Anna was going to a party. She was all ready. She had on her new pink silk dress, a ribbon round her hair, her shoes in a bag and a clean handkerchief in her pocket. She felt so excited, for she loved parties almost better than anything else.

'Now, it's time you started,' said Mother. 'Goodbye, Anna. Have a lovely time – and remember to say thank you very much to Mrs Jones when you leave.'

'I won't forget!' said Anna happily. She ran down the garden path and out into the lane. What fun it was to be going to a party! Little Louise Jones's birthday fell in Easter week this year, and it was going to be a lovely party, with an Easter egg for everyone to take home. Anna felt very happy.

She skipped down the lane past Mrs White's house. Anna always stopped and looked over the gate at Mrs White's, because she had two lovely Persian cats – blue-grey, with great orange eyes and long thick fur. Anna loved all animals – and wasn't it a pity, she had no pet of her own at all! No dog, no cat, not even a goldfish, lived at Anna's house. No one had thought of letting her have a pet. Anna's mother was not very fond of animals, so she didn't bother about them.

Anna looked over Mrs White's gate, hoping to see one of the lovely Persian cats somewhere in the garden. They loved Anna and always came running to her to be stroked. Anna knew that they had six little kittens just now – and how she longed to see them! But Mrs White was rather a grand sort of lady, and Anna didn't like to ask her if she might go and see the kittens.

There were no cats in the garden at all, so Anna went on her way down the lane, thinking of the party, and wondering if there would be red or yellow jelly, and which she would choose. Halfway down the lane she passed an old tumbledown barn – and as she went by it she heard a noise that made her stop in surprise.

It was the mewing of cats! Now what could they be mewing for in the barn? Anna stopped and looked round. She saw a curious sight! One of Mrs White's Persian cats was coming slowly along under the hedge – and in its mouth it carried one of its kittens! It was holding the kitten by the skin of its neck, as cats do. Anna was so surprised. She watched the cat slip under the hedge, make its way through the wet field and disappear into the old barn.

The mewing still went on. Anna couldn't understand it. *Mrs White's cat must have taken all her kittens into the barn*, she thought. *What a dreadful place to take them – so damp and cold and dirty! Poor little things!*

Anna found a hole in the hedge and squeezed through it. She went to the barn and peeped in. It was dark and at first she could hardly see anything. Then she discovered where the kittens were.

The mother cat had climbed up a plank, and had put all her six kittens, one by one, on a shelf in the barn. There was a hole in the barn wall just there, and the wind came in. The kittens were cold and frightened. One crawled about the shelf – and then, to Anna's horror, it fell over the edge, bounced on the plank, and rolled to the ground!

It didn't seem to be hurt, but Anna was worried. Suppose they all fell off? Silly mother cat, to put her kittens there!

Oh, dear, I shall be late for the party, thought Anna, *and I've got my best dress on. Whatever am I to do? I simply can't leave those kittens there.*

She looked around for a ladder. There was an old one at the end of the barn. Anna dragged it across and put it up against the wall. She went up it and reached the shelf where the kittens were. There were five there – and one on the floor. The mother cat was there too, and she purred when she saw Anna. Anna took hold of a kitten and carried it down the ladder. Then up she went again, and before long all six kittens were safely on the ground.

Then the little girl found an old basket, without a handle. She carefully put the kittens into it, and, with the mother cat trotting beside her, she went out of the barn and back to Mrs White's house.

How delighted Mrs White was to have her kittens back again, safe and sound! She was hunting for them everywhere!

'A dog came into the house and

frightened the mother cat,' she told Anna. 'So I suppose she thought she had better take her kittens somewhere else. They would all have caught cold in that draughty barn. It *is* good of you to take so much trouble, Anna.'

'I love all animals,' said Anna, 'especially kittens. I'd love to have a pet of my own. Oh, dear, look at my party dress! It's all dirty and I've torn it! I can't go to the party, I'm afraid!'

'Oh, I *am* sorry,' said Mrs White. 'Can't you go home and put another dress on?'

'I've only got my school dress besides this,' said Anna. 'It doesn't matter. I don't mind missing the party if I've rescued your kitten family! I do love them so much!'

So Anna missed the party, for she didn't want to go in her old school dress. She was very sad about it, and Mother was sorry for her. Mrs White had told Mother how kind Anna had been, so she understood all about it.

'Never mind, darling, you shall have an Easter egg,' said Mother, so Anna looked forward to that. She wondered if it would be a chocolate one. She did like chocolate very much.

There *was* a chocolate egg for her – and another egg too – a most surprising Easter egg! Mother brought it into the dining room with such a funny smile on her face. It was an *enormous* cardboard egg, red, yellow and blue – and it made a noise!

It did really! And what sort of a noise do you think it made? Guess!

It *mewed*! Anna gave a scream of excitement and split the egg in half – and out jumped the dearest, prettiest little Persian kitten you ever saw! It was one that Anna had rescued from the barn that week!

'Mrs White said that you were just the right person to have one of her kittens,' said Mother. 'Do you like your Easter egg, Anna?'

'Mother, it's the loveliest one in all the world!' cried Anna. 'Oh, I don't mind missing the party if I have a kitten of my own. I am *so* happy!'

Wasn't it a surprising Easter egg?

The Lonely Rabbit

Benny was a toy rabbit. He was nearly as large as a real rabbit, and he was dressed in pink striped trousers, a blue spotted coat, a bright orange scarf and tight blue shoes. So he looked very smart indeed.

But Benny was a lonely rabbit. He belonged to Lucy, and she *would* keep leaving him about everywhere. She left him in the greenhouse one night, all by himself. The next night she left him in the summerhouse and spiders walked all over his whiskers and made a web on his pretty blue shoes.

'This is horrid,' said Benny to himself. 'Lucy will keep leaving me alone in these nasty dark places. Why doesn't she remember to take me indoors to the nursery at night, when she goes to bed? She might know that I would like to talk to the other toys. It's a lonely life to be left by myself all day and all night.'

Once or twice Lucy did remember to take Benny indoors and then he was happy. But usually she left him on a garden seat or on the swing, when she went indoors to bed, and then poor Benny was lonely and frightened.

One night Lucy took Benny out into the field just outside her garden. She sat him down beside her and then began to read a book. In a little while some big drops of rain began to fall and Lucy looked up at the sky.

'Goodness!' she said, getting up in a hurry. 'There's a storm coming! Just look at those big grey clouds!'

She ran to the garden gate, opened it and rushed up the garden path. Poor Benny was left sitting in the field!

The rain fell faster and faster. The sky darkened and night came quickly. Benny's coat was soaked through and his pink striped trousers began to run, so that a pink patch showed on the grass around him. His tight blue shoes shrank and burst right off his feet.

'This is dreadful!' said Benny. 'I shall catch a dreadful cold. *A-tish-oo! A-tish-oo!*'

The rain pelted down and Benny sneezed again. '*A-TISH-OO!*'

There was a rabbit hole just behind Benny. A sandy rabbit suddenly poked the tip of his nose out and said, 'Who's that sneezing? Do come inside out of the rain.'

Benny turned and saw the rabbit. He got to his feet and went to the hole. 'Thank you very much,' he said. 'Do you live here?'

'Of course,' said the rabbit, backing

down the hole to make room for Benny. 'This is my home. I say! How wet you are! You *will* catch cold!'

Benny walked down the hole. He was wet and shivering, and he certainly didn't feel very well. The rabbit took him to a cosy room lined with moss and dry leaves.

Another rabbit was there, and she looked at Benny in surprise.

'What are you?' she asked.

'A toy rabbit,' said Benny, and sneezed again. '*A-tish-oo!*'

'Goodness, what a cold you've got!' said the second rabbit. 'I think I'd better get Pixie Lightfoot here. She can look after you till your cold is better.'

The first rabbit went to fetch the pixie. She came running in, a merry-eyed creature, with dancing skippitty feet.

'*A-tish-oo!*' said Benny.

'Goodness, what a dreadful cold!' said Lightfoot. 'Bed's the only place for you. Come with me!'

He followed her down a dark passage and at last came to a cosy room in which were chairs, a table and two small beds.

'Now, undress quickly, and get into bed,' said Lightfoot. 'I'm going to put the kettle on the fire and make you a hot drink.'

Benny took off his dripping pink trousers, his blue coat and his orange scarf. Then he got into the cosy bed and waited for his hot drink. Oh, it *was* good! It warmed him all over.

'Now lie down and go to sleep,' said Lightfoot. 'Goodnight!'

'Good – *a-tish-oo* – night!' said Benny – and in two minutes he was fast asleep.

He was much better in the morning but Lightfoot wouldn't let him get up. No, he must stay in bed until his cold and sore throat were better. She had dried his scarf for him and she tied it round his throat. 'That will keep your throat warm,' she said. 'Now here is some warm milk for you.'

It was lovely to be looked after like that. Benny did enjoy it. It was quite different from being left about by Lucy, who didn't care about him at all. He had plenty of visitors. Both the rabbits came that he had seen the night before, and all their pretty little children. A mole came too and told him a great many stories. Everything was lovely.

Three days later Lightfoot said he could get up. 'It's a fine sunny day,' she said. 'You can go out of the burrow and sit in the sunshine for half an hour.'

'But suppose Lucy comes to look for me,' said Benny in alarm. He didn't at all want to go back to her.

'Well, you silly, just pop down the hole again like the other rabbits do,' said Lightfoot. 'You needn't put on your coat and trousers – they have shrunk and are far too small for you – but you must keep on your orange scarf because of your throat.'

So out into the sunshine Benny went, and it was so lovely and warm there that he fell fast asleep. And while he was asleep Lucy came and found him. She lifted him up and looked at him.

'Well!' she said. 'I wonder if this can be Benny. I left him here – but where are his shoes – and his pretty trousers and lovely blue coat? It can't be Benny – but this is his scarf round his neck, that's certain! Except for that he looks very like a real rabbit!'

Just then Benny woke up. He opened his eyes and looked at Lucy. What a shock he got! He struggled and leapt down to the ground. Lucy pounced after him – but he was down the hole in a twinkling, and Lucy couldn't catch him.

It can't have been Benny! she thought. *It must have been a rabbit that had stolen Benny's scarf – and to think I nearly took him home. Oh, I do wish I could find Benny. I'd never leave him about again if only I could find him.*

But she never did find him – for Lightfoot told Benny he could live with the other rabbits if he liked, and do just as they did. 'It only needs a little magic rubbed into your fur to make you just like them,' she said. 'I'll do it, if you like.'

So she did – and Benny became a real

live rabbit like all the rest, as happy as the day was long, with plenty of company and lots to do all the year round.

But Lightfoot made him wear his scarf always, because his soaking had given him a very weak throat, and as soon as he left off his scarf he caught a cold. He always remembers to put it on when he goes out of the burrow, and as it is a very bright orange, it is easy to see.

So if ever you see a rabbit playing on the hillside, with an orange scarf tied round his throat, you'll know who he is – Benny! But don't tell Lucy, will you?

The Easter Chickens

Tommy was staying with Auntie Susan and Uncle Ben at the farm for Easter. Mummy and Daddy had gone away for a holiday by themselves, and Tommy was sorry because he did so like Easter at home. There were coloured Easter eggs on the breakfast table to eat then – and chocolate ones too – and perhaps a fluffy yellow chick tied to one egg, or a little rabbit.

I don't expect Auntie Susan or Uncle

Ben know what a little boy likes at Easter*, thought Tommy. *I don't expect they will buy me any eggs at all. I wish I was at home with Mummy and Daddy!*

Sure enough, when Easter morning came and Tommy ran downstairs to breakfast, there was no coloured egg for him in his eggcup – only just an ordinary brown egg laid by Henny-Penny, the brown hen.

Tommy looked to see if there were any chocolate eggs for him – but there wasn't even a very small one. He felt very sad.

'Sit down and eat your breakfast, Tommy,' said Auntie Susan. 'We must get on because I have a lot of things to do today.' Auntie Susan always had a lot of things to do. So did Uncle Ben. Perhaps that was why they hadn't remembered his Easter eggs, Tommy thought. He remembered how he had seen a little yellow chick in the sweetshop yesterday down in the village. It was carrying an egg. He would have liked that very much. He wondered if he should ask Auntie Susan if she would buy it for him, but he decided that he mustn't ask for things. She said if he was nice enough, people would always buy him things because they loved him, without being asked.

I may not have been nice enough, Tommy thought. So, instead of being sulky and disappointed, he tried to be extra nice to Auntie Susan, and ate his egg without dropping a single bit of the yellow part on the tablecloth.

'Can I go on any errands for you, Auntie Susan?' he asked, when he had finished breakfast.

'I think Uncle Ben wants you to go down to the hen-coops with him,' said Auntie. 'I'm coming too.'

So they all three went down to the hen-coops. There were four of these, with four brown hens sitting on thirteen eggs each.

And do you know, when they came to the first hen-coop, some of the eggs had hatched! Yes – and there were three yellow chicks running about saying,

'Cheep-cheep-cheep!' as loudly as they could.

'Oh!' said Tommy, delighted. 'Look at those dear little chicks, Auntie! Do look at them! They are much sweeter than the toy ones I saw in the shop yesterday! And oh, look – they have got something tied to their backs – whatever are they carrying?'

'Look and see,' said Uncle Ben with a laugh.

So Tommy crouched down and peeped to see what they were carrying. The chicks had gone into the coop with their mother and it was difficult to see one.

At last one of them came out again – and what *do* you suppose it had got on its back? A little chocolate egg! Fancy that!

'It's carrying an egg, just like the little chick at the sweetshop!' cried Tommy. 'Oh, who is the egg for, Auntie Susan?'

'It's for a nice little boy I know, called Tommy,' said Auntie Susan, laughing. 'That chick has an egg from *me*, Tommy – and that one has an egg for you from Uncle Ben – and the third one has an egg from Mummy and Daddy. It came for you yesterday, and we kept it till Easter Day. Then when the chicks hatched out, we thought you would like to have eggs and chicks together – really proper Easter chicks this time!'

'Auntie! Are the yellow chicks for me as well? Oh, I am *so* pleased!'

Uncle Ben caught the chicks and took off the chocolate eggs for Tommy. The little boy cuddled the soft cheeping chicks. Their little bodies were so warm. He loved the tiny creatures – and they were his very own!

'Will they grow into hens and lay me eggs?' he asked.

'Oh, yes!' said Auntie Susan. 'You shall take them home with you next week when you go – real, live Easter chicks, Tommy, for your very own!'

'This is the nicest Easter I've ever had,' said Tommy. 'And I thought it wasn't going to be. What *will* Mummy say when I take home my Easter chicks!'

Tommy still has his chicks – but they are growing into brown hens now and will soon lay him eggs – one for his own breakfast each morning, one for his mummy, and one for his daddy. Don't you think he is lucky?

The Top of the Wall

Greeneyes lived in a little cottage surrounded on all sides by a high red wall. He liked to be sheltered from the winds – and from prying eyes; for Greeneyes was half a wizard!

Next door to him lived Dame Fiddlesticks and her children. Dame Fiddlesticks was a most inquisitive person and loved to peep at her neighbours. If she went into her bedroom she could just see nicely over the wall into the old man's garden. That *did* annoy him! And then the children took to climbing on the top of the wall and calling to him. That annoyed him more than ever!

At last he decided that he must do something about it. If he had the wall made higher by a foot, Dame Fiddlesticks couldn't see into his garden from her bedroom window and the children wouldn't be able to climb up and sit on top. So off he went to Mr Hod the builder.

'Yes,' said Mr Hod. 'It would be easy to do what you want – but you will offend Dame Fiddlesticks mightily. She might throw her rubbish over your wall in revenge, and her children would certainly call out after you when you go walking, for they are not very well-mannered. Take my advice and think of something else. It is usually just as possible to get your way in a kindly manner as in an ill-natured one.'

Greeneyes nodded his head and went to see his cousin, Mother Tiptap. She heard what he had to say and smiled. 'I've just the thing for you!' she said. 'See, here are some new seeds I have made. Plant them on the top of your wall and see what happens.'

'But no seeds will grow on a *wall*,' said Greeneyes. Still, he took them and planted them all along the top of his wall. Then he waited to see what would happen. The rain came. The sun shone. Those tiny seeds thrust out roots into the wall-crannies. They sent up small leaves. They grew and they grew.

And then one day in the springtime they flowered bright yellow and red – tall plants, over a foot high, with the most delicious scent in the world! Greeneyes smelt them from his kitchen window and was glad. Dame Fiddlesticks feasted her eyes on them, for she loved flowers, and when she smelt their scent she was full of joy.

'Don't you dare to climb up on that wall any more!' she warned her children. 'I won't have those beautiful flowers spoilt that that kind man has planted there. They've grown so high that I can't peep into his garden any more, but what does that matter? I'd rather see the flowers there!'

She was so delighted that she sent in a new cake she had baked to the man. He went to thank her and asked what he could do in return for her kindness.

'Oh, if only you'd give me a few seeds of those lovely flowers of yours growing on the wall,' she said. 'What are they called?'

'They've no name at present,' said the old man, smiling. 'What shall we call them? Let's ask the children.'

The children knew what to call them, of course! Do *you* know the name?

Gillian and the Lamb

Once upon a time Gillian went down to the farm to fetch some eggs all by herself.

'I shall take my doll Betty with me,' she said to her mother. 'She has had a bad cold, and the sunny air will do her good. I shan't be long, Mummy.'

So Gillian tucked her doll up well, put her purse with the egg money under the cover of the pram, and set out down the lane, feeling rather proud to think she was out by herself.

She went over the bridge and peeped at the brown stream underneath. She saw a great many white daisies in the grass, and some early buttercups. She heard a lark singing so high up in the sky that she couldn't see him at all.

'I hope you are enjoying this nice walk,' she said to Betty, her doll, who was sitting up with her woolly hat on her curly hair.

Soon Gillian came to the farm. There were so many hens running about that she had to be quite careful where she wheeled her doll's pram. They said 'Cluck, cluck!' to her in loud, cheerful voices, and she said 'Cluck, cluck!' back. It was easy to talk hen language.

She wheeled her pram up to the farm door. She knocked. Nobody came. She knocked again, a bit harder this time. Still nobody came.

'Oh, dear!' said Gillian. 'That means no one is in – and I shall have to go home without the eggs. What a pity!'

So she set off home again. She had just passed the field where the big haystack stood when she saw something moving in the hedge. She stopped to see what it was.

'Oh, it's a tiny baby lamb!' said Gillian in surprise. 'It's escaped from the field. Go back, lamb! If you don't, a car may come along and knock you down.'

But the lamb wouldn't go back. It came

limping over to Gillian, and then she saw that it had torn its leg on the barbed wire that ran along the hedges there. She knelt down and looked at the leg.

'When I hurt my leg, I have it bathed and some good stuff put on it,' said Gillian. 'Your mother sheep can't do that – but perhaps she will lick it better if you go back to her. Look – there she is, peeping through the hedge at you!'

Sure enough there was a big mother sheep putting her head through the hole in the hedge, baaing loudly. Gillian picked up the tiny lamb and carried it back to the hole – but it wouldn't go through it! It kept limping back to Gillian.

'Whatever shall I do with you, lamb?' she said. 'I can't leave you here in the lane. And you won't go back to your mother. And there is no one at the farm this morning to look after you.'

She stared at the lamb and the lamb stared back at Gillian. 'Maa-aa-aa!' said the lamb in a small, high voice, and it wriggled its tail like a hazel catkin on the hedge.

'I shall take you home to my own mother,' said Gillian. 'She is kind and will know what to do with you. She will make your leg better.'

'Maa-aa-aa!' said the lamb.

'Come along then,' said Gillian. 'Walk close behind me, lamb.' But the lamb wouldn't. It just stood there in the middle of the lane, maaing and wriggling its tail.

'Well, really, I don't know what to do with you!' said Gillian. And then an idea came into her head. Of course! She could wheel the lamb in her pram! It was quite small enough to go in.

So she picked up the tiny lamb, and put it gently in the pram beside Betty, the doll. 'I'm afraid you will be a bit squashed, Betty,' said Gillian. 'But I can't help it. Lie down, lamb. I'll cover you up nicely.'

The lamb was surprised to find himself in a pram. He lay quite still. Gillian covered him up. She tucked him in well in case he wriggled loose. 'Maa-aa-aa!' said the lamb, and he sniffed at Betty, the doll.

Gillian wheeled the pram up the lane. She met Mr Logs, the woodman. 'Good morning,' he said. 'And how's your doll today?'

'She's a bit squashed because she's sharing the pram with a lamb,' said Gillian. Mr Logs bent to see – and when he saw the little lamb looking at him, how he laughed!

'That's a funny sight!' he said. 'Well, well, well!'

Then Gillian met Mrs Thimble, who did sewing for lots of people. 'Good morning, Gillian,' she said. 'And how's your doll today?'

'She's a bit squashed because she's sharing the pram with a lamb,' said

Gillian. Mrs Thimble bent down to see, and how she laughed when the little lamb said 'Maa-aa-aa!' to her.

'No, *I'm* not your ma-aa-aa!' she said. 'I can hear your ma baaing for you in the field!'

'Oh, there's my mummy!' said Gillian. 'I must go and show her my lamb. Goodbye!'

She wheeled the pram in at the gate of Old Thatch. Her mother was weeding a bed nearby. She called her.

'Mummy! Here's a lamb with a hurt leg! It wouldn't go back into its field – and there's no one at the farm – so I've brought it home for you to mend.'

Her mother stood up in astonishment

and looked for the lamb. She didn't think of looking into the pram!

'Where *is* the lamb?' she said.

'Maa-aa-aa!' said the lamb, waving one of its feet over the pram cover. How Gillian's mother laughed! She laughed and she laughed to see the lamb lying in the pram with Betty, the doll.

'Whatever will you do next, Gillian?' she said. She took the lamb out of the pram and looked at its leg.

'Go and get me a basin of water,' she said. So Gillian ran off. Very soon the lamb's leg was washed and some good stuff put on it. It wasn't very bad. It didn't even need a bandage, though Gillian badly wanted to put one on.

Just then the farmer's wife came by the gate, home from shopping, and she looked in. How surprised she was to see the lamb in the garden of Old Thatch!

Gillian told her all about it, and the farmer's wife laughed when she heard about the lamb being wheeled in the pram.

'Thank you for being so kind as to look after it for me,' she said to Gillian. 'I'll carry it back to the field now, and mend the fence.'

So she did – but always after that, when Gillian went down the lane, the little lamb watched for her and maa-ed to her. It put its tiny head through the hedge, and you may be sure that Gillian always stopped to rub its little black nose!

The Big Box of Chocolates

Peter Penny had been very good to Dame Twinkle when she had hurt her foot and couldn't go out to do her shopping. He had run her errands every morning for a week, and she was very grateful.

'I want to give you a present, Peter Penny,' she said. 'I wonder what you'd like. You have been very good to me.'

'I don't want anything, thank you,' said Peter Penny, who had been very well brought up and knew that it was wrong to expect presents for kindness.

'Well, I'm going to give you something,' said Dame Twinkle, who had also been well brought up and knew that she must certainly show Peter Penny how pleased she was with his kindness to her. 'How would you like that big box of chocolate animals that is in Mrs Peppermint's sweetshop?'

'Ooh!' said Peter Penny, his eyes opening wide. The big box of chocolate animals was perfectly lovely. All the little folk of the village had gone to look at it and had longed to have it. If Peter Penny had it, he could give a party and his friends could all share the animals. It would be really lovely.

Dame Twinkle saw Peter's eyes shining brightly, so she at once went to Mrs Peppermint's shop and bought the box of chocolate animals. Then she gave it to Peter Penny with her love.

He had a large net bag with him, because he had to do his shopping that morning, so he thanked Dame Twinkle very much indeed, and put the box into his bag. Then off he went to do his shopping. He bought bacon and sausages, a pound of rice, a tin of cocoa, some flowers and a new saucepan. Everything was squashed into his big net bag and soon it felt very heavy.

Peter Penny went home through the Magic Wood. When he was halfway through, something dreadful happened. The bottom of his net bag broke into a hole, and out fell the big box of chocolate animals on to the soft grass. Peter Penny was swinging the bag as he went and singing a very loud and merry song, so he didn't know what had happened. The saucepan in the bag stopped anything else from falling out. Peter Penny went happily on, not knowing at all that he had lost his precious box of chocolates.

Now not very far behind him came Mrs Twitter, who sold yellow canaries in her little shop. Always when she came through the Magic Wood she wished a wish, because sometimes wishes came true there. And today she wished her wish.

'I do wish I could find a nice present lying on the ground all waiting for me!' she wished.

And, dear me, the very next moment what should she see on the ground but the big box of chocolate animals that Peter Penny had dropped! She gave a squeal of surprise and rushed at it in delight.

But when she saw what it was her eyes filled with tears. 'Chocolate!' she said. 'Oh, dear, what a pity! Chocolate always makes me feel so sick. Whoever would have thought I'd find a box of chocolates when my wish came true!'

She picked up the box and carried it off. As she went she wondered what to do with it.

I know, she thought. *I'll give it to Mr Ho-Ho. He's been ill in bed for a long time now, and I'm sure he would love to have a nice box of chocolate animals.*

So she went to Mr Ho-Ho's, and left the box with the maid, who at once took it to Mr Ho-Ho.

He opened the box, and, dear me, how his face fell when he saw what was inside.

'Chocolates!' he groaned. 'Would you believe it? Just what the doctor said I wasn't to have! What very bad luck! Oh, bother, bother, bother!'

He lay and looked at them. Then he thought that it would be a very good idea to send the box to Silvertip, the elf across the way. It was her birthday and he would like to send her something. He knew she was very fond of chocolates.

So he sent his maid with the big box across the way, and she knocked at the door. 'A present from Mr Ho-Ho,' she said when Silvertip opened the door. The elf screamed with delight and ran indoors with it. But, dear me, when she saw what it was, she sighed and sighed.

'Look!' she said to her elfin husband. 'Another box of chocolates! That makes the fifteenth I've had today for my birthday. Whatever shall I do?'

'Well, if you don't want it, don't waste it,' said her husband. 'Let me take it to Mother Hooky for her little boy. He'll love all these chocolate animals.'

'But he's such a very, very *naughty* little boy,' said Silvertip, who didn't like the small boy at all.

'Never mind,' said her husband. 'Naughty or good, he'll like chocolates.' So off he went and gave the box to Mother Hooky for Hoppy, her small magical brownie son.

She was pleased – but what a pity, when Hoppy came home from school he was so rude and naughty that she really could *not* give him the chocolates. She sent him straight to bed instead.

She sat and looked at the box. 'What shall I do with them?' she wondered. 'I can't eat chocolates myself, and if I leave them in the cupboard that naughty little boy will steal them. I know! I'll give them to that nice Peter Penny. He has been so good to Dame Twinkle lately, running all her errands for her, and I know he likes chocolates.'

So she went to Peter Penny's house. Nobody was in. There was no light anywhere. So Mother Hooky opened the kitchen window and popped the box on the table just inside. She smiled to herself and thought, *I won't tell Peter Penny what I've done. He can just find them and wonder where they've come from!*

Now when Peter Penny had got home that morning, he had emptied his net bag on the table and looked for the box of chocolates at once. He thought he would like to eat one of the chocolate bears. They did look so very nice.

But to his great disappointment and horror there was no box there! It was gone. Then he saw the big hole in the bottom of the bag and he guessed what had happened. How upset he was!

'What bad luck!' he said to himself. 'To lose that wonderful box of chocolates – the best one I've ever had in all my life! Oh, dear, I suppose I must go all the way back through the wood to see where I've dropped it.'

Poor Peter Penny! He had his dinner and then off he went to see if he could find his lovely box of chocolates. He looked here and he looked there, he hunted in the wood, he hunted in the fields. But no matter how hard he looked there was no box of chocolates to be seen. It was quite gone.

Peter Penny was tired and miserable. He couldn't help a few tears squeezing out on to his cheeks as he went home. He was very nearly home when he met Smarty the gnome, who thought himself very clever indeed.

'What's the matter, Peter Penny?' asked Smarty, staring at Peter's tears in surprise.

'Oh, nothing,' said Peter.

'Tell me what's the matter,' said Smarty, who was always curious to know everybody's business. 'Has someone been teasing you?'

'Of course not!' said Peter.

'Well, what's the matter then?' asked Smarty, simply longing to know.

So Peter Penny told him all about how he had been kind to Dame Twinkle, and how she had given him the wonderful box of chocolates, and how he had lost them.

'It's the first reward I've ever had for being kind,' said Peter sadly, 'and now I've lost it.'

'Oh, that's the way of the world,' said

Smarty at once. 'It doesn't pay to be kind, you know, because you hardly ever get anything back for it, and if you do, you're bound to lose it. No, my boy, you listen to my advice. Don't go bothering to do kind deeds. Just get what you can out of other people, and look after yourself! It doesn't *pay* to be kind and good.'

'It certainly doesn't seem to,' said Peter Penny. 'It's very hard to lose that lovely box of chocolates. I shan't bother to be kind to anyone again.'

He said goodbye to Smarty and went on. He hadn't gone very far when he saw old Mr Candleshoe, almost bent double under a big load of wood. Now Peter was really a very kind fellow and his first thought was to go and help Mr Candleshoe.

Then he stopped himself. *No*, he thought, *I won't. Why should I help him? I shan't get anything out of it. As Smarty says, kindness doesn't pay.*

So he went right past Mr Candleshoe, and didn't even say 'good afternoon'.

But no sooner had he passed him than Peter Penny felt bitterly ashamed of himself and he went as red as a sunset sky. *How horrid of me!* he thought. *Am I so mean that I can't give a hand to an old chap like Candleshoe? What do I care if kindness is rewarded or not? I shall be kind because I want to be!*

So back he went and took Candleshoe's big bundle away from him. He carried it all the way home for him and then turned to go to his own cottage.

'You're a kindly fellow!' called Candleshoe after him. 'A rare, kindly fellow, you are, Peter Penny. May you get what you most want today!'

Peter Penny smiled a crooked little smile. *What I most want is that perfectly lovely box of chocolate animals*, he thought. *But that's gone for good*.

Then he stopped in the greatest astonishment, for there, set on the kitchen table, was the very box of chocolates he had lost that morning. There it was, with no note, no message.

How did it get there? Where did it come from? What a very extraordinary thing!

'Ooh!' said Peter Penny in delight, picking it up. 'Ooh! Who says kindness isn't rewarded!'

He danced round and round the room in joy, and a chocolate bear fell out of the box. Peter Penny picked it up and ate it. It was delicious.

'Now to write out the invitations to my chocolate party!' cried the little fellow happily. 'What fun we shall have!'

And when all his friends came to the party, Peter Penny told them about the very mysterious way in which the box of chocolate animals had appeared in his kitchen, and they were really most astonished.

'You deserve all the good luck you get,' said his friends, hugging him. I think he does too, don't you?

How Very Surprising!

'I've planted my seeds!' called Sandra. 'And I've put labels in to show what they are.'

Mother came to look at Sandra's little garden. It had one rose tree in it and a pansy plant. The rest of it was bare brown earth, where Sandra had planted her seeds.

'You'll have to water them if the weather stays dry, Sandra,' said Mother.

'But I haven't a watering can,' said Sandra.

'You can borrow Pat's – ask him if you may,' said Mother, so Sandra went to ask her big brother.

'Can I borrow your watering can, Pat, to water my seeds when they grow?' she asked.

'No, you can't,' said Pat, looking up from his book. 'I lent you my scissors and you lost them. And I lent you my new book and you tore a page. I'm not lending you anything else.'

'I bought you some *new* scissors!' said Sandra. 'And it wasn't my fault the book got torn – I just left it open on the table and the kitten got up and scratched at the page.'

Pat said nothing. He just went on

reading. Sandra ran off to find her little basket. She would weed all round the edges of her garden and make it look neat!

Her seeds soon came up. She saw them in little green rows and patches and felt very pleased. The ground looked very dry because there had been no rain, and Sandra wondered if she should water her seedlings.

'Yes, of course,' said Mother.

'But Pat won't lend me his watering can,' said Sandra. 'I asked him.'

'Well, that's rather selfish of him,' said Mother. 'You can't possibly hurt his can – or even lose it!'

'Can I use Daddy's?' asked Sandra.

'No, dear – it's far too heavy,' said Mother. 'Let me see now – what *could* you use?'

'What about the old nursery teapot?' said Sandra. 'The spout's broken off halfway and the lid is broken too – and you said you couldn't get it mended, so it's never used now. Could I take that to water my seedlings with? It would be just about right for them.'

Mother laughed. 'What an idea – to water your garden with a teapot! Yes, I don't see why you shouldn't take it, dear – I shan't use it any more now. Keep it for yourself.'

Sandra was pleased. She ran off to get the teapot with the broken spout. She was glad to use it because she had always loved it. It had rabbits and chicks all over it, and she was sure it was sad because no one ever used it now.

She went down the path to the garden tap and filled the little teapot. Then she carried it to her garden and watered all her green seedlings carefully. The teapot dripped cold water gently over them, and Sandra thought how pleased they must be to have a drink when they were so thirsty.

'I'll leave you here, in the long grass by my garden,' she said, and put the teapot down there. 'Then Pat won't see you and take you away and hide you. He isn't always very kind, you know.'

The teapot settled down in the long grass. Pat didn't see it when he came by. He noticed that Sandra's garden had been watered, and wondered if she had used his can. He went to ask her.

'No, I *didn't* borrow your can,' said Sandra.

'But you've been watering your garden!' said Pat. 'What did you use to water it with then?'

'I shan't tell you!' said Sandra. 'It's something Mother gave me, Pat – something we used to use in the nursery – but it's mine now.'

'If we used to use it in the nursery, then it's partly mine,' said Pat. 'What is it? I might not want you to use it.'

But Sandra wouldn't tell him, and he went off crossly. He didn't guess that it was the little nursery teapot, hidden so cosily in the long grass.

The weather was very wet after that. It rained nearly every day, and Sandra didn't have to water her garden at all, so the teapot was quite forgotten. Sandra's seeds grew and grew, and some of them even put out tiny buds. She was very pleased.

Then the weather became hot and sunny, and Sandra thought she really must water her plants again. Now, where had she put that old teapot without a lid?

'Oh, yes – in the long grass beside my

garden bed,' she said and hunted for it. 'Ah, here it is, but oh, it's full of something! Who could have put all this mess inside it?'

Just as she was bending down to pick it up a tiny blue and yellow bird flew round her head. '*Pim-imim-imim!*' he said. '*Pim-imim-imim!*'

'What do you want, blue tit?' said Sandra, surprised. 'Oh, you dear little bird, why are you singing at me like that?'

The blue tit suddenly darted down to the teapot – and went in at the little hole where once the lid had been! Sandra stared in astonishment.

'Why, surely you haven't a nest in there?' she cried. 'You have, you have!

Oh – in the old *teapot* – and your front door is where the lid went!'

She peered down and there was the little blue and yellow tit sitting right in the teapot, on the 'mess' inside – but it wasn't a mess; it was a nest!

Sandra could hardly believe her eyes. She raced up in the garden, shouting at the top of her voice.

'Mother! The blue tits are nesting in our garden – and guess where!'

'In my nesting box?' shouted Pat hopefully.

'No! It's nowhere near your nesting box!' cried Sandra. 'Mother, come and see!'

So down the garden went Mother, and Pat ran too. Where *were* the blue tits nesting? Pat had hung up a lovely nesting box for them that he had made himself – and now after all they had nested somewhere else!

'Look, Mother – there's the nest!' said Sandra, pointing down to the teapot. 'In the old nursery teapot you gave me for watering my garden. See – the mother bird is sitting right inside! She gets in through the lid hole.'

'Well! How lovely!' said Mother. 'What a peculiar place to choose – but tits always love to nest in holes of any kind. How lucky you are, Sandra!'

'You ought to share the nest with *me*, because the nursery teapot was as much mine as yours,' said Pat, jealous because he had so badly wanted the tits to nest in the box he had made.

'All right,' said Sandra generously. 'You can share it. I don't know how many eggs are in it – but half can be yours. Oh, to think we'll have heaps of tiny blue tit babies!'

The blue tit flew out of the hole in the teapot, and Sandra peeped in. 'One, two, three, four, five, *six* eggs!' she said. 'Three for each of us. When will they hatch, Mother?'

'I don't know,' said Mother. 'Fairly soon, I expect. But don't disturb the tits too often, Sandra, or you may make them desert the nest.'

'But I'll *have* to water my garden!' said

Sandra. 'See how dry it is, Mother. Oh, but I *can't* water it now!'

'Why not?' asked Mother.

'Well, because the tits have got my watering can, of course!' said Sandra. 'I was using it for a watering can, don't you remember?'

'Dear me, yes,' said Mother. She looked straight at Pat, and he went red.

'You can use *my* can, Sandra,' he said. 'But I'm not sorry I wouldn't lend it to you before!'

'Now, Pat, don't be unkind, just after Sandra has said you can share the nest,' said Mother.

'I'm not!' said Pat. 'All I mean is, if I *had* lent Sandra my can instead of saying 'no', she wouldn't have used the nursery teapot – and so the tits wouldn't have been able to nest there – and we wouldn't have had any baby blue tits. That's all!'

'Oh, well then, *I'm* glad too that you wouldn't lend me your can!' said Sandra. 'But I'm glad that I can use it *now*, Pat – because the blue tits need the teapot more than my seedlings do!'

The eggs have all hatched now, and the old teapot is full to overflowing with tiny blue and yellow birds. I do wish you could see them!

The Big Juicy Carrot

One fine morning, Bobtail, the rabbit, met Long-Ears, the hare, and they set off together, talking about this and that.

They stopped by a hedge and lay quiet, for they could hear a cart passing. Bobtail peeped through and saw that it was a farm cart, laden with carrots and turnips. How his mouth watered!

And then, just as the cart passed where the two animals were crouching, a wheel ran over a great stone, and the jerk made a big, juicy, red carrot fall from the cart to the ground. The hare and the rabbit looked at it in great delight.

When the cart had gone out of sight the two of them hurried into the lane. Bobtail picked up the carrot. Long-Ears spoke eagerly. 'We both saw it at once. We must share it!'

'Certainly!' said Bobtail. 'I will break it in half!'

So he broke the carrot in half – but although each piece measured the same, one bit was the thick top part of the carrot, and the other was the thin bottom part. Bobtail picked up the top part – but Long-Ears stopped him.

'One piece is bigger than the other,' he said. 'There is no reason why *you* should have the bigger piece, cousin.'

'And no reason why *you* should either!' said the rabbit crossly.

'Give it to me!' squealed the hare.

'Certainly *not*!' said the rabbit. They each glared at the other, but neither dared to do any more.

'We had better ask someone to judge between us,' said the hare at last. 'Whom shall we ask?'

Bobtail looked all round, but he could see no one but Neddy the donkey, peering over the hedge at them.

'There isn't anyone in sight except silly

Neddy,' he said. 'It's not much good asking *him*. He has no brains to speak of!'

'That's true,' said Long-Ears. 'He is silly, everyone knows that. But who else is there to ask?'

'No one,' said Bobtail. 'Well, come on. Let's take the carrot to the donkey and ask him to choose which of us shall have the larger piece.'

So they ran through the hole in the hedge and went up to Neddy. He had heard every word they said and was not at all pleased to be thought so silly.

The two creatures told him what they wanted.

'If I am so silly as you think, I wonder

you want me to judge,' said Neddy, blinking at them.

'Well, you will have to do,' said the rabbit. 'Now tell us – how are we to know which of us shall have the bigger piece?'

'I can soon put that right for you, even with *my* poor brain!' said Neddy. He took the larger piece in his mouth and bit off the end.

'Perhaps that will have made them the same size!' he said, crunching up the juicy bit of carrot he had bitten off.

But no – he had bitten off such a big piece that now the piece that *had* been the larger one was smaller than the other!

'Soon put *that* right!' said Neddy, and he picked up the second piece. He bit a large piece off that one, and then dropped it. But now it was much smaller than the first piece!

The hare and the rabbit watched in alarm. This was dreadful!

'Stop, Neddy!' said Long-Ears. 'Give us what is left. You have no right to crunch up our carrot!'

'Well, I am only trying to help you!' said Neddy indignantly. 'Wait a moment. Perhaps *this* time I'll make the pieces equal.'

He took another bite at a piece of carrot – oh, dear, such a big bite this time! The two animals were in despair.

'Give us the rest!' they begged. 'Do not eat any more!'

'Well,' said Neddy, looking at the last two juicy pieces, and keeping his foot on them so that the two animals could not get them, 'what about my payment for troubling to settle your quarrel? What will you give me for that?'

'Nothing at all!' cried Long-Ears.

'What! Nothing at all?' said Neddy in anger. 'Very well then – I shall take my own payment!'

And with that he put his head down and took up the rest of the carrot! Chomp-chomp-chomp! He crunched it all up with great enjoyment.

'Thanks!' he said to Long-Ears and Bobtail. 'That was very nice. I'm obliged to you.'

He cantered away to the other side of the field, and as he went, he brayed loudly with laughter. The two big-eyed creatures looked at one another.

'Bobtail,' said Long-Ears, 'do you think that donkey was as silly as we thought he was?'

'No, I don't,' groaned Bobtail. 'He was much cleverer than we were – and you know, Long-Ears, if one of us had been sensible, we would *both* now be nibbling carrot – instead of seeing that silly donkey chewing it all up!'

They ran off – Bobtail to his hole and

Long-Ears to the field where he had his home. As for Neddy, he put his head over the wall and told his friend, the brown horse, all about that big juicy carrot.

You *should* have heard them laugh!

Fairy Easter Eggs

Once upon a time there lived an uncle and aunt who didn't believe in fairies. They lived on the edge of a wood, and though Ben and Mary, their nephew and niece, knew perfectly well that the wood was simply *full* of fairy folk, Uncle John and Aunt Judy said it was all nonsense.

'But we *saw* two little gnomes only yesterday,' said Ben. 'Truly, Uncle. They were running by the hazel trees.'

'Stuff and rubbish!' said Uncle John.

'And, Auntie, I played with a fairy all yesterday morning!' said Mary.

'Fiddlesticks!' said Aunt Judy, who was busy cooking. 'Don't tell stories.'

Ben and Mary said no more. They ran off into the garden and began to play. If only Uncle John and Aunt Judy had believed in fairies, they would have been quite happy. Hollyhock Cottage was a jolly place to live in, and there were lots of chickens to feed and flowers to pick.

Sometimes Ben and Mary fed the hens themselves, and they always fetched in the eggs. Aunt Judy let them have a new-laid egg every morning for breakfast. She used to choose the brownest eggs for them because she thought they tasted the nicest of any.

So you see Aunt Judy was really very kind.

'If *only* she wouldn't keep saying there aren't any fairies,' sighed Mary. 'Even if she's never seen one herself, that doesn't *prove* there aren't any!'

'Of course it doesn't,' said Ben. 'And if Uncle John knew how often he nearly catches a fairy when he chases butterflies and moths for his collection, he *would* be surprised!'

'Let's go and tell the fairies about it,' suggested Mary. 'We've got nothing else to do, and there's half an hour before tea.'

Off they ran into the wood. When they came to a little sunken dell, they sat down beneath some hazel trees. No fairies were about, it seemed, but Ben and Mary knew that the little folk only come when mortals are quiet and peaceful.

They kept a sharp lookout, and presently Mary spied one peeping from beneath some violet leaves. Then Ben saw one dressed in grey, swinging on the pussy willow, and soon, as the children kept quite still, a score more little peeping heads showed from behind toadstools and tree trunks.

'It's only Ben and Mary!' cried a shrill little voice suddenly, and the pussy willow fairy flew down beside the children. Then out ran a dozen others, and down flew more still, until a chattering, skipping little group surrounded Ben and Mary.

'Why didn't you come and play yesterday?'

'Why didn't you come earlier today?'

'Why do you look unhappy?'

The fairies called out their questions in little high voices, and some of them climbed on to Mary's knee.

'We're not *really* unhappy,' said Mary. 'But you see, Uncle and Aunt don't believe in fairies, and they say we tell stories about you.'

'And that makes us sad, of course,' said

Ben, 'because we *don't* tell stories about you or anything else. We always talk truly, don't we, Mary?'

'Couldn't you somehow or other make Uncle or Auntie know about you?' asked Mary. 'Couldn't you all suddenly fly into Auntie's kitchen or something?'

Ben giggled. 'That *would* give her a surprise!' he chuckled. 'Or couldn't you take turns at sliding down Uncle's newspaper in the mornings?'

The fairies shook their heads. 'We're not allowed to show ourselves to people who don't believe in us,' they answered.

'Oh, please,' begged Mary. 'Please! Remember how we helped you to find those two little lost fairies last summer, and how often we have brought you honey from our beehive.'

The pussy willow fairy put his hands in his pockets, and began to speak.

'I was one of those lost fairies,' he said. 'I don't mind helping you if someone else will join me.'

Another little fairy crept from behind a daffodil, where she had been listening to all that went on.

'I was the other lost fairy,' she said in a tiny little voice. 'I'll help you too.'

'Splendid!' said Ben in delight. 'Now the thing is – what shall we do?'

'They ought to hide somewhere and then suddenly fly out when Auntie and Uncle are near,' said Mary.

'Yes – something like that!' said Ben. 'Let's think hard!'

Everybody thought for two minutes.

Then Ben suddenly lifted his head and smiled.

'Could you get inside an egg?' he asked the willow fairy.

'Easily,' answered the fairy in astonishment.

'Well, listen!' cried Ben. 'We have the two brownest eggs every morning for breakfast. Can you by magic get inside the two brown eggs we'll have, so that when we crack them in the morning we'll find you there curled up, alive and real?'

'Oh, *then* we could show you to Auntie

and Uncle, and they'd know!' cried Mary. 'They'd know it was magic too, to get inside an *egg*!'

'We can make two very brown eggs by using a spell,' said the willow fairy slowly. 'But if we get inside them and ask the other fairies to carry us to your hen's nest, will you promise that no harm shall come to us tomorrow morning, when you have opened the eggs?'

'Yes, yes, we promise you!' cried Ben and Mary gladly. 'Will you do it then?'

'Yes, we will,' answered the two fairies. 'We'll be there tonight in the two brownest eggs. Carry us carefully when you take us in!'

The two children ran off feeling most

excited. Aunt Judy and Uncle John would soon believe in fairies!

They were just in time for tea. They said nothing of where they had been, but they longed for the time to come when Aunt Judy would send them out to bring in any eggs laid since the morning.

'Just run and bring in the eggs,' she said at last.

Off the children ran. They raced down the path to the henhouse, and lifted up the lids of the nesting boxes.

'One, two, three, four, five, six, seven eggs, Mary!' cried Ben. 'And look at these two brown ones! They must be the magic ones. How exciting!'

'You'd better carry those two, Ben,' said Mary nervously. 'I'll carry the others. *Do* be careful of the fairy eggs.'

Ben was tremendously careful of them. He carried one in each hand, and walked slowly up the path to the kitchen door.

He put the eggs in a basket on the table, and Mary carefully put the others in too.

'Seven eggs, Auntie,' she said in rather a shaky voice, 'and two of them are *very* brown.'

'You shall have those for breakfast then,' said Aunt Judy. 'Now run away. I'm going to be busy.'

Off they went, full of excitement, to

think of what would happen next morning.

But they had forgotten that the next day was Easter Sunday.

Aunt Judy had bought two fine chocolate Easter eggs for them, and as she looked at the hens' eggs that the children had brought in an idea came to her.

'I'll paint all the eggs for tomorrow's breakfast just as my mother used to do when *I* was a child!' she decided. 'There's something very exciting about coloured eggs on Easter Sunday! Let me see – two for Uncle John, one for Ben, one for Mary, and one for me! What fun it will be!'

She quickly got her cochineal out of the cupboard to make the eggs red. Then she decided that it would make them look very colourful if she used Uncle John's purple ink and some of his green ink. She fetched them.

The eggs began to look so colourful! They had red at the top and bottom, stripes of green and crosses of purple here and there.

'Won't Ben and Mary be pleased!' chuckled Aunt Judy, and put them carefully on a shelf to dry.

'But, dear me!' she said, as she stood looking at them. 'They're so bright with colours that I really can't tell which were the two brown ones I promised Ben and Mary! Never mind, it won't matter for once!'

Next morning the two children ran hurriedly downstairs to breakfast.

'Come along, dears,' said Aunt Judy, 'your eggs are all ready.'

Ben and Mary looked at their plates – then they looked again – then they rubbed their eyes and stared hard.

'What's happened to the eggs, Auntie?' asked Mary at last in an astonished voice.

Aunt Judy laughed at their surprise, and began to pour out tea.

'It's Easter Sunday, so I thought you should have colourful Easter eggs!' she said. 'They're all painted, look!'

Ben and Mary saw that their uncle's

and aunt's eggs were just as colourful, and they began to feel relieved.

'I thought some of the magic had gone wrong,' Mary whispered to Ben.

'Eat your eggs, children,' said Aunt Judy, opening her letters.

'Now for it!' whispered Ben. He took his spoon and Mary took hers.

Crack-a-crack-crack!

They gently tapped the eggshell and cracked it. They took it off and laid it on their plates.

Then they stared at each other in the greatest disappointment and astonishment, for the eggs were proper ones, with white and yolk – no fairies were there at all!

Tears came into Mary's eyes, and Ben looked gloomy.

'The fairies must have been afraid at the last minute,' he said to his sister. 'Cheer up, Mary, and eat your egg. We'll think of another idea.'

Just then Uncle John began to crack *his* egg. He took off the shell top and peered in surprise. He felt for his glasses and put them on his nose. Then he stared again at his egg.

'Judy, my dear,' he said at last to his wife.

'What, John?' asked Aunt Judy.

'This egg's *bad*,' said Uncle John.

'Dear, dear, dear, but it *can't* be,' said Aunt Judy. 'Why, it was only laid yesterday.'

'Well, there's nothing in it except a little mess at the bottom,' said Uncle John in disgust.

Then an astonishing thing happened. Out of the egg flew a tiny fairy, and shrieked at Uncle John in an angry voice.

'I'm *not* a little mess, I'm *not* a little mess!'

Uncle John started back in astonishment.

'Bless my buttons!' he cried. 'It's a squeaking butterfly! I must catch it for my collection!'

Directly the fairy heard that she gave a cry of fright and flew straight out of the window.

Ben and Mary sat watching in the greatest astonishment.

'The eggs have got mixed!' suddenly wailed Mary.

'Mixed! What do you mean, *mixed*?' asked Aunt Judy, who was lost in amazement at the sight of something flying out of one of her new-laid eggs.

'Oh, Auntie, I'll show you!' said Ben. 'Please will you let me crack the other two eggs that are left?'

'And Uncle,' said Mary, 'please put that horrid net away for just a minute.'

Uncle John, thoroughly puzzled, let it fall on to the floor.

Then Ben carefully cracked one of the

remaining two eggs. No, it was a proper one. He reached for the other.

Crack-a-crack!

It was a fairy egg!

Down at the bottom lay the little pussy willow fairy curled up tightly, looking at Ben with wide frightened eyes.

'My goodness gracious!' sighed Aunt Judy, her face flushing red with astonishment and delight. 'Did ever you see such a beautiful wee creature! What is it?'

'A fairy!' said Ben. 'Look, Uncle!'

Uncle John stared hard into the egg. He was very short-sighted, so perhaps that explains his mistake.

'Call it a fairy or anything you like,' he

said. '*I* call it a butterfly, and how it got inside that egg is a marvel and a mystery to me. But if you're set on its being a fairy, I won't say anything more! Your eyes are better than mine!'

He picked up his net to put it away. But the fairy thought he was going to catch him, and he flew straight up in fright just as Uncle John bent over the egg once more.

Bump he went into Uncle John's nose, and sent his glasses clattering on to the table! Then out of the window he flew, and disappeared among the trees outside.

'That was a very *solid* butterfly, anyway!' said Uncle John in surprise.

Aunt Judy didn't say much. She just ate

her rolls and honey, and thought. Ben and Mary didn't dare to say anything either. As for Uncle John, he kept wondering out loud all breakfast what sort of butterflies those 'egg things' were.

But after breakfast Aunt Judy called Ben and Mary to her, and gave them the lovely chocolate eggs she had bought for them.

'Here you are,' she said. 'Take them out into the wood and play with the fairies.'

So you see they *knew* she believed in them from that very morning, and they ran off as happy as could be.

But you *should* just have heard the fairies storming because one of them had been called a 'little mess', and both had been called butterflies! It took Ben and Mary a long time to make them pleased again.

And then how they laughed to hear that the pussy willow fairy had bumped Uncle John's spectacles off!

The Blackbirds' Secret

Did you know that the blackbird family have a secret that they never tell any other bird or any other creature?

Hundreds of years ago the Prince of White Magic wanted to mend his Well of Gold. This was a strange and curious well, which had always been full of pure golden water. Anything that was dipped into this water became as bright and shining as gold, and was beautiful to see. But, because of so many, many years of usage, the well water had become poor and no longer seemed to have the golden power it once used to have.

So the prince decided to go to the Land of Sunlight, and buy enough pure golden rays to make his well golden again. He set off, taking with him a special thick sack so that the sunlight would not be able to shine through the sack and so give away his secret. He bought what he wanted, and by his enchantment imprisoned the sunny gold in the sack. He tied it up tightly and set off home again.

But somehow his secret journey to the Land of Sunlight became known, and the Yellow-Eyed Goblins, who lived in the Dark Forest, decided to waylay the prince as he passed through their kingdom and rob him of the sack. Then they would use it for the Dark Forest, and make it light and beautiful.

Now the prince had made himself invisible, but he could not make the sack unseen. Also, much to his dismay, he found that it was not thick enough, after all, to stop the golden rays from shining through. He would very easily be seen in the Dark Forest. What was he to do?

He called a blackbird to him and asked his advice, and the bright-eyed bird thought of a splendid idea at once. He would ask each blackbird in the forest to spare a black feather from his wing and, with the help of the sticky glue that covered the chestnut buds on the trees, they would stick the dark feathers all over the sack, and so hide the brightness inside.

In a second this was done. The blackbirds dropped their feathers beside the prince and he rubbed each one in chestnut glue. Soon he had entirely covered the sack with the black feathers, and it was impossible to see it in the darkness of the gloomy forest. He passed safely through the kingdom of the Yellow-Eyed Goblins, for not one of those crafty little creatures caught a glimpse of either the prince or his black-feathered sack.

The sunlight gold was emptied into the old well, and at once the water gleamed brightly. Anything dipped into it became a shining orange-gold, beautiful to see. The prince was delighted. He called the kind blackbirds to him and spoke to them.

'You have helped me,' he said, 'and now I will reward you. All birds like to be beautiful in the springtime. You may make your big beaks lovely to see – so when the springtime comes near, blackbirds, fly to this well and dip your beaks into the golden water. Then you will have bright, shining beaks of orange-gold.'

And every year since then the

blackbirds have flown in springtime to the secret golden well, and have come back to us with shining golden beaks.

The Blown-Away Rabbit

There was once a small rabbit who was a very friendly creature. His name was Bobbin, and if you could have seen his white tail bobbing up and down as he ran, you would have thought this name was a very good one!

He lived just outside the farmyard, near the pond where the big white ducks lived. He used to play with the yellow ducklings, and they were very fond of him.

One day Waggle-Tail, the smallest duck, had a terrible fright. He ran away from the others, because he wanted to see if there was a puddle he could swim on all by himself. The pond seemed so crowded when all the white ducks and the yellow ducklings were on it.

Well, Waggle-Tail waddled off to where he saw the rain puddle shining. It was a very nice puddle indeed. Waggle-Tail sat on it and did a little swim all round it, quacking in his small duckling voice.

The farm cat heard him, and left his seat on the wall at once. Young ducklings made wonderful dinners for cats – but usually the ducklings kept with the big ducks, and the farm cat was afraid then.

'A duckling on a puddle by itself!' said the big grey cat to himself in joy. He crept round by the wall. He crept round the pigsty. He crouched low and waggled his body ready to jump – and just then the duckling saw him. With a terrified quack he scrambled off the puddle and ran to find his mother.

But he went the wrong way, poor little thing. He went under the field gate instead of under the gate that led to the pond. The cat crept after him, his tail swinging from side to side.

'Quack! Quack! Quack!' cried the yellow duckling. 'Quack! Quack! Quack!'

But his mother didn't hear him. Nobody heard him – but wait! Yes –

somebody *has* heard him! It is Bobbin the little rabbit!

Bobbin heard the duckling's quacking, and popped his long ears out of his burrow. He saw Waggle-Tail waddling along – and he saw the farm cat after him.

'Waggle-Tail, Waggle-Tail, get into my burrow, quickly!' cried Bobbin. Waggle-Tail heard him and waddled to the burrow. The cat would have caught him before he got there, if Bobbin hadn't leapt out and jumped right over the cat, giving him such a fright that he stopped for just a moment.

And in that moment the little duckling was able to run into the rabbit's hole!

Down the dark burrow he waddled, quacking loudly, giving all the rabbits there *such* a surprise!

Bobbin leapt into the hole too, and the friends sat side by side, wondering if the cat was still outside.

'I daren't go out, I daren't go out,' quacked poor Waggle-Tail.

'I will go and fetch your big white mother duck,' said Bobbin. 'I can go out to the pond by the hole that leads there. Stay here for a little while.'

Bobbin ran down another hole and up a burrow that led to the bank of the pond. He popped out his furry head and called to Waggle-Tail's mother.

'That cat nearly caught Waggle-Tail.

He is down my burrow. Please will you come and fetch him.'

So the big white duck waddled from the pond and went to fetch her duckling from Bobbin's burrow. She was very grateful indeed to Bobbin for saving her little Waggle-Tail.

'Maybe some day I shall be able to do you a good turn too,' she said. And off she went, quacking loudly and fiercely at the farm cat, who was now lying in the sun on the wall.

Now not long after that, Bobbin wanted to go and see Waggle-Tail – but when he put his nose out of the burrow he found that it was raining very hard indeed.

'You must not go out in that rain,' said his mother. 'Your nice fur will be soaked. Wait till it stops.'

But it didn't stop. The rain went on and on and on. Bobbin was very cross. *I will borrow an umbrella*, he thought. So he went to his Great-Aunt Jemima, and was just going to ask her for an umbrella when he saw that she was fast asleep, with her paws folded in her shawl. But there was the big red-and-green umbrella standing in the corner!

Bobbin knew that no one should borrow things without asking, but he simply couldn't wait until Aunt Jemima woke up. So the little rabbit tiptoed to the corner and took the big old umbrella.

He scuttled up the burrow with it, dragging it behind him. He pulled it out of the hole and put it up. My goodness, it *was* a big one!

Bobbin held on to the big crook handle and set off down the hillside. It was a very windy day, and the big purple clouds slid swiftly across the sky. A great gust of wind came, took hold of the umbrella – and blew it up into the sky!

And Bobbin went with it! He was such a little rabbit that the wind swept him right off his feet with the umbrella – and there he was, flying along in the sky, holding on to the umbrella!

He was dreadfully frightened. He clung to the handle with his two paws, hoping that he wouldn't fall, but feeling quite sure that he would, very soon. Poor Bobbin!

The wind swept him right over the pond. The ducklings looked up in surprise when they saw the enormous umbrella – but how they stared when they saw poor Bobbin hanging on to it too!

'It's a rabbit, it's a rabbit!' they cried.

And Waggle-Tail knew which rabbit it was. 'It's Bobbin, my dear friend Bobbin!' quacked Waggle-Tail. 'Mother, Mother, look at Bobbin! He will fall. What can we do to save Bobbin? He saved *me* – we must save *him*!'

'But how can we?' said the mother duck.

'Mother, can't you fly after him?' cried Waggle-Tail. 'I know you don't often fly, because you prefer to swim – but couldn't you just try to fly after poor Bobbin?'

'I will try,' said the big mother duck. So she spread her big white wings and rose into the air. She flapped her wings and flew after the big umbrella. Bobbin was still holding on, but his paws were getting so tired that he knew he would have to fall very soon.

The mother duck flew faster and faster on her great wings. She caught up the umbrella. She flew under the surprised rabbit and quacked to him.

'Sit on my back! Sit on my back!'

Bobbin saw her just below him. He let go the umbrella handle and fell neatly on to the duck's broad, soft back – plop! He held on to her feathers.

Down to the pond she went, carrying the frightened rabbit. What a welcome the little ducklings gave him! As for Waggle-Tail, he could hardly stop quacking!

'You did me a good turn, and now my mother has paid it back!' he quacked. 'Oh, I'm so glad you're safe!'

'So am I,' said Bobbin. 'But, oh, dear, what about my Aunt Jemima's umbrella? It's gone to the clouds!'

It came down again the next day, and fell into the field where Neddy the donkey lived. Neddy took the handle into his mouth and trotted to Bobbin's burrow with it.

'Here you are!' he said to Bobbin. 'I heard that your Aunt Jemima might punish you for taking her umbrella without asking. I hope she hasn't.'

'No, she hasn't,' said Bobbin joyfully. 'Oh, thank you, Neddy! What good friends I have!'

He ran down the burrow with the big umbrella, meaning to give it to his Great-Aunt Jemima. But she was asleep again, with her paws folded in her shawl, so Bobbin quietly stood the umbrella in the corner and ran off to tell Waggle-Tail.

'Don't get blown away again, will you,

Bobbin?' begged the duckling. And Bobbin promised that he wouldn't. He didn't want any more adventures just then!

A sparkly collection of short stories
for six-year-olds from the world's
best-loved storyteller!

A wonderful collection filled
with adventure and magic for
seven-year-olds from the world's
best-loved storyteller!

ENIDBLYTON.CO.UK
IS FOR PARENTS, CHILDREN AND TEACHERS!

Sign up to the newsletter on the homepage for a monthly round-up of news from the world of

Enid Blyton

JOIN US ON SOCIAL MEDIA

Enid Blyton

is one of the most popular children's authors of all time. Her books have sold over 500 million copies and have been translated into other languages more often than any other children's author.

Enid Blyton adored writing for children. She wrote over 700 books and about 2,000 short stories. *The Famous Five* books, now 80 years old, are her most popular. She is also the author of other favourites including *The Secret Seven*, *The Magic Faraway Tree* and *Malory Towers*.

Born in London in 1897, Enid lived much of her life in Buckinghamshire and loved dogs, gardening and the countryside. She was very knowledgeable about trees, flowers, birds and animals.

Dorset – where some of the Famous Five's adventures are set – was a favourite place of hers too.

Enid Blyton's stories are read and loved by millions of children (and grown-ups) all over the world. Visit enidblyton.co.uk to discover more.

Illustration by
Laura Ellen Anderson.